Editorial by Alexandra West
Designed by Joe Merkel

MGM

THE ADDAMS FAMILY © 2019 Metro-Goldwyn-Mayer Pictures Inc. © 2019 Metro-Goldwyn-Mayer Studios Inc. All Rights Reserved.

METRO-GOLDWYN-MAYER is a trademark of Metro-Goldwyn-Mayer Lion Corp. © 2019 Metro-Goldwyn-Mayer Studios Inc. All Rights Reserved.

Manufactured in China. No part of this book may be used or reproduced in any manner whatsoever without written permission except in the case of brief quotations embodied in critical articles and reviews. For information address HarperCollins Children's Books, a division of HarperCollins Publishers, 195 Broadway, New York, NY 10007.

"ADDAMS FAMILY THEME" by Vic Mizzy
Published by UNISON MUSIC COMPANY (ASCAP)
Administered by NEXT DECADE ENTERTAINMENT, INC.
All Rights Reserved Used by Permission.

www.harpercollinschildrens.com
Library of Congress Control Number: 2019938805
ISBN 978-0-06-294679-9

19 20 21 22 23 SCP 10 9 8 7 6 5 4 3 2 1

First Edition

METRO GOLDWYN MAYER PICTURES Presents "THE ADDAMS FAMILY"
Based on Characters Created by CHARLES ADDAMS
Distributed through UNITED ARTISTS RELEASING
© 2019 Metro-Goldwyn-Mayer Pictures Inc. All Rights Reserved.
The Addams Family™ Tee and Charles Addams Foundation. All Rights Reserved.

THE ADDAMS FAMILY

SNAP

SNAP

Music and Lyrics by Vic Mizzy
Illustrations by Lissy Marlin

HARPER
An Imprint of HarperCollinsPublishers

They're creepy

and they're kooky,

mysterious and spooky,

they're altogether ooky,

...the Addams Family.

Their house is a museum,

...the Addams Family.

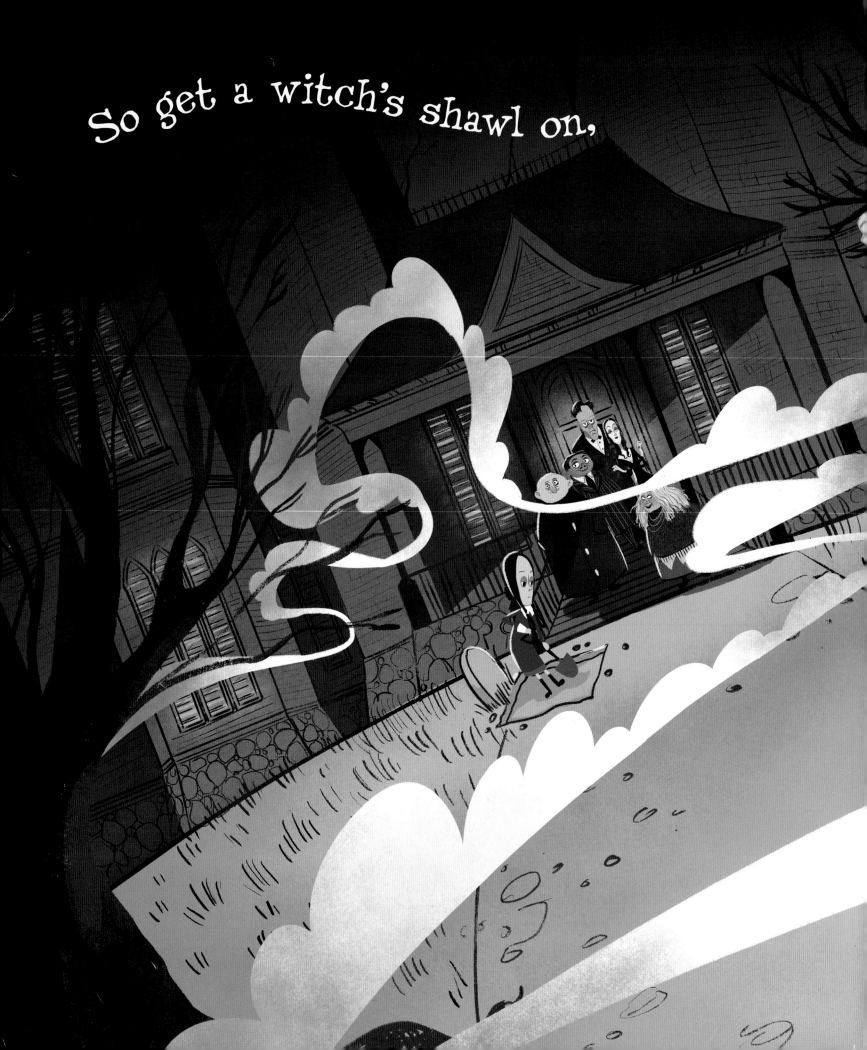

So get a witch's shawl on,

a broomstick you can crawl on,

we're gonna pay a call on